KB063448

True Freedom

The One Thing that Happy People
Have in Common

True Freedom

The One Thing that Happy People
Have in Common

Ven. Pomnyun Sunim

Translated by Juyoung Yoo and Youngtae Choi

JUNGTO

True Freedom

by Ven. Pomnyun Sunim

JUNGTO Publishing
1585-16, Seocho-3dong, Seocho-gu, Seoul, South Korea / +82-2-587-8991
4361 Aitcheson Rd. Beltsville, MD 20705 USA /+1-240-786-7528

Website : www.jungto.org
email : book@jungto.org

Printed in South Korea
First Edition : Summer, 2011
Second Edition : Summer, 2013

ISBN 978-89-85961-68-4 03810

CONTENTS

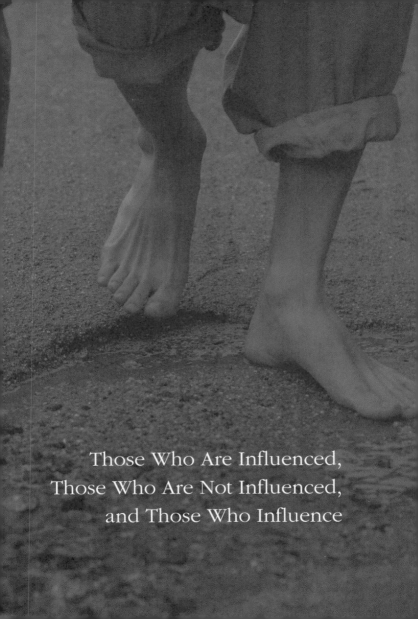

Those Who Are Influenced,
Those Who Are Not Influenced,
and Those Who Influence

Those Who Are Influenced, Those Who Are Not Influenced, and Those Who Influence

Four Categories of People

You could say that there are four categories of people, depending on the way they respond to the world around them. In the first category are people who are easily influenced by negative external conditions. In the second category are those who are not influenced by their surroundings because they distance themselves from negative circumstances. In the third category are those who are not influenced despite being in the midst of such conditions. Finally, in the last category are those who influence others; not only are they not influenced by negative external conditions but rather change them into positive ones.

Those Who Are Influenced By External Conditions

What kind of people are those who are influenced by external conditions? They are people who, if they live with a friend who drinks, begin to drink before they realize it; if they live with a husband who angers easily and uses foul language, they soon become like him; if they live with someone who sleeps in every day, they do the same; and if they live with a greedy person, they also become greedy. Bad habits are easily learned; we embrace them without being aware of them. Many of us fall into this category.

When you ask people the reason for acquiring bad habits, they answer, "Do you think I wanted to learn these bad habits? It happened naturally simply by living with him/her." It's the story of our lives. We go to elementary school because others do. It's the same with high school and college. We get a job and get married simply because others do so. Also, if our neighbor buys a house or a car, we feel compelled to do the same. People seem to lead independent lives, but actually they mostly follow the actions of others without even realizing it.

Young adults who did not drink until graduating high school begin drinking when they go to college because their friends drink, and also begin smoking because their friends smoke. They begin these behaviors simply because they feel uncomfortable not doing what everyone else is doing. They blindly follow other people's actions. These are "sentient beings" or ordinary people.

Individuals widely reported in the media as participants in corrupt scandals often defend their actions, arguing that they thought it was okay to do the things they did. They are not particularly bad people; they were simply following the actions of their predecessors. That's why these people feel little guilt. When they fall under investigation, they feel they are unjustly accused and think, 'Everybody does it but gets away with it. Why am I so unlucky?'

Ordinary people are easily influenced by external conditions. This is the reason that Mencius' mother moved three times in search of a good educational environment for her son.* Between good and bad influences, people are more susceptible to the latter. People learn bad habits more quickly. It is not because learning positive behavior is especially difficult. It is simply because bad habits are extremely common, so people are more prone to learning them and thinking they are acceptable.

* Mencius is a Chinese philosopher who is regarded as the most famous Confucian after Confucius.

In the second category are the people who are not influenced by external conditions as they distance themselves from them. They don't associate with friends who drink or smoke. They don't live with people who use foul language. Buddhist monks fall into this category. They sever ties with people with bad habits and avoid associating with them. As the English saying goes, "He that touches pitch shall be defiled." People in this category avoid anything or anyone that can influence them negatively. Because these people keep themselves free of bad habits and negative behaviors, they are described as being "clean, pure, sublime, and noble."

The people in the first category highly respect those in the second category, to the point that the former group deifies and idolizes the latter. However, despite their respect and admiration, the people in the first category do not follow the example of those in the second. When asked why they do not do so, they answer, shaking their heads, "How can people live like that?" However, they greatly admire those in the second category. Although the people in the first category do not want to live like those in the second category, they tell others to do so. They explain the reasons they don't do it themselves, saying "If everyone lived like that, the world would not go around." It is as if they continue with their bad habits and negative behaviors out of concern for the world. They think highly of those in the second category, but they don't want to live like them, which shows their double standards.

The people in the first two categories can be grouped together in the sense that they are in danger of being influenced by external conditions. Whether they accept or reject these circumstances, they are dependent on them. While the people in the first category are bound by the belief, "I cannot help living like others," those in the second category are equally bound by the idea, "I must not live like others." In other words, the first group is trapped by their desires, while the second is held captive by their quest to avoid external conditions. To put it another way, the former group is confined to their homes, while the latter, which retreated to the mountains, is confined to the mountains. The people in the first category are fenced in by the thought, 'What's the fun of living if people don't eat meat and drink alcohol?' while those in the second category are restricted by the notion, 'I must not eat meat or drink alcohol.'

Those Who Are Not Influenced by External Conditions

In the third category are the people who are not influenced by external conditions. They don't drink or smoke, even though they hang out with friends who do. Nor do they become greedy, despite living among greedy people. They are Mahayana bodhisattvas. Only when people reach this stage can they talk about being "free." We say that being obsessed with desire is the same as being bound by circumstances. Because people in the third category are liberated from desires, they are free from external conditions. They are neither swayed by any external condition nor influenced by any situation.

Figuratively speaking, the people in the first category are those who went out to sea on a boat, were washed overboard by big waves, and are frantically calling for help and struggling to stay alive. They are the people who marry someone they love but soon become unhappy in their marriages; at work, they clash with coworkers; and when they get home, they have conflicts with their wives or husbands, parents, and children. As a result, they get angry, irritated, resentful, distressed, and lonely.

The people in the second category can be compared to those who have built a levee to keep out the waves and lead safe and peaceful lives inside it. When they quietly looked into their minds after suffering many difficulties, they realized that they fought with their families over trivial things. Their relationships with coworkers were not very good either. So, after much internal struggle, they severed all their family and social ties and left home to live in the mountains or deep in the woods. Now, they no longer suffer because of their work or other people. They say, "Now, no one can bother me. My mind is at ease." However, their lives can be compared to rowing a boat on a tranquil lake, trapped inside a levee.

One group of people is desperately struggling to stay afloat at sea, while the other is aboard a boat on a tranquil lake. It might seem like the two groups are in extremely different situations; however, that is not actually the case.

The people in the first category feel a temporary happiness between waves. When a wave hits, they are immersed in the sea. Then when the wave passes, they can raise their heads to the surface and breathe. They feel happy for an instant before another wave hits them. Similarly, in life, people alternately experience suffering and happiness from moment to moment.

The people in the second category also experience suffering and happiness alternately. The only difference is that their suffering and happiness are bigger in scope and longer in duration than those experienced by the people in the first category. However strong the levee may be, it will eventually be broken by strong and continual waves. Then, the people in the second category will be plunged into the sea. Even if the levee does not break, the reality is that they are trapped inside it and cannot move one step out of it. They may enjoy what seems to be freedom inside the tiny lake, but that is not true freedom.

The people in the third category build a big boat, learn how to row it and put up the sail in order to make effective use of the wind and the waves to navigate it. They sail the seas to their hearts' content, unhindered by weather conditions. If it's windy, they sail the boat using the

force of the wind. And if there are big waves, they use the strength of the waves to sail the boat, precariously keeping their balance. They are not affected by any external conditions. Some people might say that they have attained complete freedom or Nirvana. However, they have not reached absolute happiness or freedom. They have yet to attain "true freedom," which is the ultimate goal of practice.

Those Who Influence External Conditions

The people in the first, second, and third categories have one thing in common. Those in the first are suffering because they have fallen into the sea against their will; those in the second have built a levee so that they won't fall into the sea; and those in the third are freely sailing the seas on a big boat, without falling in, despite strong winds and high waves. The common thread is that people in all three categories consider avoiding a fall into the sea as happiness. Then, what kind of people are those who are in the fourth category? These people do not give a thought to "not falling into the sea." It doesn't really matter to them whether or not they fall. The people in the first three categories are bound by the thought that they are happy if they don't fall into the sea. However, those in the fourth category are happy whether or not they take such a plunge. What do they do when they fall into the sea? They gather pearl oysters, as would a diver who intentionally submerses himself.

Many people go into the sea. Divers collect clams or sea cucumbers, while adventurers look for treasure. When they dive for sea cucumbers and pearl oysters, divers have not unintentionally tumbled into the sea but have gone below water to do their jobs. If by chance the people in the fourth category fall in while sailing, they gather some clams while there. Falling into the water is not a distressful event for them. Like those who deliberately go into the sea, they might as well pick some clams during their time below the surf. For them, it's good whether they fall in or not. They don't consider such an occurrence a particularly unpleasant event.

To use another analogy, the people in the first category are those who drive cars, get into accidents, damage their vehicles, injure themselves, and run up huge medical bills. Those in the second category never drive a car for fear of an accident. They won't be in an accident, but they can't get around either. Those in the third category are good drivers and don't get into accidents even if they drive on busy and dangerous roads. For those in the fourth category, it doesn't matter whether or not they get into an accident. If by chance they do wreck and hit their heads hard on the steering wheel, they realize at that instant, 'Death can occur at any moment. If so, is it really worth fighting over the things we hold onto dearly in our lives?' With this realization, the car accident turns out to be a blessing in disguise, an epiphany which might not have happened had it not been for the accident.

To reiterate, the people in the first category are those who keep making mistakes when they shouldn't; those in the second, to ensure that they don't fail, don't do anything; those in the third don't make a single blunder whatever they do; and those in the fourth don't mind whether or not they make an error. When they make a mistake, they learn even more than they would have had they not messed up. You need to understand this fourth category to be able to comprehend the meaning of enlightenment or Nirvana achieved by the Buddha.

Taking a cursory look, it is hard to distinguish between the people in the first category and those in the fourth. The people in the second category are completely different from those in the first, so it is easy to tell them apart. Those in the third category might be a little hard to distinguish from those in the first category, because they live together in the same environment. However, upon careful observation, it is easy to tell them apart because those in the third category are unusual.

They don't get angry when someone swears at them and do not drink while hanging out with people who do; they don't behave at all like ordinary people. However, the people in the fourth category behave in the same way as those in the first category, so the two groups are almost impossible to tell apart.

Using another analogy, the people in the second category don't befriend anyone who drinks, and those in the third category have friends who drink but they themselves don't drink. Then, how do those in the fourth category behave? They hang out with friends who drink and drink along with them, so it's virtually impossible to distinguish them from real drinkers. However, after a couple of months, their drinking buddies stop drinking.

When a woman in this category lives with a husband who uses foul language, she uses foul language toward him as well, but after about six months to a year, the husband stops doing so. When people in the fourth category live with greedy people, the latter group soon stops being greedy. Also, when they hang out with wrongdoers, they misbehave along with them, but after a while, the latter group of people is transformed.

The people in the fourth category influence external conditions. They are not afraid of being affected by negative conditions. They live among "sentient beings," embrace those with bad habits and negative behaviors, and gradually influence them positively. A wet rag cleans dirty things on

the dirty floor by absorbing all the dirt. Likewise, the people in the fourth category absorb the bad habits and negative behaviors of other people, and change them for the better.

True Freedom Is Attained Only Through Enlightenment

The only way you can attain true freedom is through "enlightenment." Therefore, practicing dharma cannot be done through modeling or following principles. You have to find your own way. Attaining enlightenment is not an adaptation to the environment, but similar to mutation. When a person changes by adapting to the environment, he or she is likely to change again when the environment changes. With continued practice, you will reach a stage in which you no longer have to worry about being changed or influenced by external conditions. When you practice with the aim of attaining Nirvana, you will go through the four different stages. Many people in the first stage will be happy just to reach the second stage. However, the ultimate goal of practice, that is, becoming a Mahayana bodhisattva, is to go beyond the third stage and reach the fourth.

Where Am I Now?

What stage of practice are you in? I recommend you practice with a clear goal in mind. If you aim for the second stage, you must change your current way of life. This requires a firm resolution and decisive action on your part. You must discontinue your current lifestyle and relationships. However, if you want to become like those in the third stage, you don't have to change your way of life. A strong inner determination is all you need. It is of no consequence to you what others around you do. You should be able to look at a person who drinks and think, 'Whether that person drinks or not is his problem.' You should have firm values guiding your life. However, if you aim to reach the second stage, you don't particularly need to have strong values. All you need to do is to leave society and live in seclusion among people with good habits. Then, you can become like them. For example, if you live with people who wake up at 4 o'clock in the morning and switch on all the lights, you have no choice but to wake up at that time. External conditions control your behavior. On the other hand, if you are in the third stage, you can control yourself regardless of your environment.

For the people in the first stage, external conditions are very important. Their environments are the determining factors in their lives. For those in the second stage, the place they choose to practice is very important, so they talk about which mountain, which Dharma teacher, or which country would be good for their practice. Like the people in the first category who roam the world seeking a comfortable life, an ideal spouse, a good job, and an interesting field of study, those in the second category search far and wide for good people, places, and books in the name of seeking "the Path."

The people in the first stage love eating, sleep whenever they get a chance, and have busy love lives; they basically try to enjoy life to the fullest. On the other hand, those in the second category are the opposite. They eat and sleep as little as possible, staying away from the opposite gender. However, those in the third category are indifferent to external conditions such as locations or circumstances of their practice. They are well aware that the root of all suffering is in the mind. Because of their firm values, they are not influenced by whether their neighbors live in a small or a big house, whether they wake up early or late in the morning, or by what they eat and what they do. They think, 'It's their life, so it's up to them. I live frugally because I like living this way. I don't have to either follow or reject the way others live.'

The people in the second stage ridicule and look down upon those in the first stage, saying, "They are foolish and crazy. No wonder they are suffering." However, the people in the third stage do not criticize the people in the first stage. They mind their own business, thinking, 'The people in the first category act that way because of their disposition and karmic consciousness.' This doesn't mean that those in the third category don't have any compassion for others. They simply think what others do has nothing do with their own practice. Rather, they react according to the situation and don't let anything hinder their practice.

The people in the fourth category don't dwell on their practice. They don't give the slightest thought to what their state of practice is, what they need to do, or how they should live. Like water, which changes its shape according to the cup that holds it, they do not insist on a course of action but simply respond to each person and situation. In Buddhism, this is called "Hwajak." Bodhisattvas transform themselves to embody billions of different beings according to the situations and karmas of the people they meet, in order to guide them toward the right path.

THE BEGINNER'S MIND

We tend to live our lives habitually.

When we try to repeat an action or behavior, we are not likely to have the same mindset we had as when we did it for the first time.

When we visit a place we have never visited before, we tend to be curious about the place.

We thus try to examine it closely and understand it.

Let us try to do the same with our lives.

Let us try to live our lives with a curious mind,

as if we were doing something for the first time,

With a new mindset and the utmost sincerity.

Master Wonhyo,
the Life of a Bodhisattva

Master Wonhyo,
the Life of a Bodhisattva

Young Wonhyo Becomes a Buddhist Monk Upon Clear Observation of Contradictions in Life

Before he became a monk, Master Wonhyo, a young man from a noble family, was a Hwarang.* He felt compelled to lead his country to victory every time he went to war and lived with the thought that he had to excel over others as a

---

* A group of elite young noble men who excelled in warfare and the arts during the Shilla Dynasty (57 BC - 935 AD).

Hwarang. If by any chance he lost a battle, he was sad and outraged, sometimes vowing revenge, and other times challenging the enemy again and winning. It was the life of those in the first category, namely ordinary people. Then, one day, one of his friends, also a Hwarang, died during a battle against Baekje, a neighboring country. Thus, he was weeping in front of his friend' s tomb, vowing to avenge his death, when it suddenly occurred to him, 'The generals and soldiers of Baekje, who killed my friend and won the war, may be toasting their victory at this very moment.' He realized that at the very instant he was mourning the death of his friend with bitter tears, the enemy camp was celebrating its victory. It also flashed through his head that when Shilla previously had won in a war and he and his friends were toasting their victories, their enemies would have been grieving the deaths of their friends and shedding tears of revenge just as he was doing.

People on one side were weeping while those on the other side were celebrating in regards to the very same event. Seeing this paradoxical nature of human life, he realized the futility of life. At that very moment, he cut his own hair and became a Buddhist monk. Then, he made his house into a Buddhist temple, naming it "Chogaesa Temple," and immersed himself in Buddhist practice.

Master Wonhyo studied Buddhist sutras diligently. The sutras contained thorough explanations given by the Buddha about the cause of suffering in human existence, as well as ways to alleviate suffering. His efforts to find truth in the sutras increased with each passing day. He was completely absorbed in the pursuit of truth, often forgetting to eat or sleep. He had sometimes been afraid to die in the battlefield, even though he fought bravely, risking his life. He now devoted himself to Buddhist practice without fear of death, even ready to die. However, he was not satisfied with his progress.

Thus, Master Wonhyo decided to go to China where he would be able to obtain more Buddhist sutras and meet great teachers. He left for China with Master Uisang. While traveling through Goguryeo, a country bordering Shilla to the north, they were captured by Goguryeo soldiers and accused of spying. They were imprisoned and almost killed before managing to escape to Shilla. However, Master Wonhyo did not give up his journey to China, and decided to travel by ship. On his way to the ship, he spent a night in a cave. In the middle of the night, feeling thirsty, he groped for something to drink in the dark and grabbed a bowl. He drank water from the bowl, and he thought it tasted very good. When he woke up the next morning, he found that the cave was in fact a tomb and the bowl he drank from was a skull. He suddenly felt sick, and at that moment, he realized, 'Ah, everything is created by the mind!' The water and the bowl were no different from those of the previous night. However, the water that had tasted so refreshing the night before almost made him vomit the next morning. This led him to realize that the problem wasn't in the water or the skull but in the mind. Thus, he sang an enlightenment song.

When one thought arises,
all things arise.
When one thought disappears,
all things disappear.
Everything is created by the mind.

He realized that this was the meaning of "everything is neither dirty nor clean," as stated in *the Heart Sutra*. With the realization that everything originates from the mind, he no longer had a reason to go to China or India, to search in the books, or roam the mountains in the quest for enlightenment. Therefore, he returned to Shilla.

After attaining enlightenment, Master Wonhyo found Buddhist sutras easier to understand and more interesting than before. At the time, different Buddhist sects in Shilla were arguing over the correct interpretations of Buddhist sutras. This was because the Buddha's teachings recorded in different sutras sometimes seemed to contradict one other. If interpreted correctly, all the sutras said the same thing and followed the same logic. However, nobody had been able to see this until Master Wonhyo.

Here is an example that can illustrate this point. Let's suppose some people asked the Buddha for directions to Dallas. In one sutra, the Buddha told them to go east; in another sutra, he told them to go north; and in another, he told them to go west. In each sutra, the Buddha suggested a different direction to people headed to Dallas. However, upon closer observation, one is able to understand that he told the people living in Los Angeles to go east, those living in Houston to go north, and those living in Washington, D.C. to go west. The Buddha gave the right directions to Dallas from the locations from which various groups of people were starting their journeys.

Thus, Master Wonhyo began to write books explaining that if people understand the core message of each sutra, disputes between various Buddhist sects over the interpretations of sutras are unnecessary. This is because, although the Buddha's teachings may have been worded differently in each sutra, they all showed people the way to become enlightened. This is the premise of Master Wonhyo's famous "Hwajaeng-sasang" (Philosophy of Reconciliation and Harmonization) and the Buddhist thought that unified all the diverse Buddhist sects in Shilla. This profound principle was too advanced to be understood and accepted in China, where there were many highly-developed Buddhist sects. At the time, each Buddhist sect in China had depth in its study of Buddha's teachings. However, being divided into many different sects, they were unable to integrate the different interpretations into a unified Buddhist thought.

When Master Wonhyo wrote *The Doctrine to Unite Ten Sectarian Opinions* and *Treatise on the*

Awakening of Faith in the Mahayana, he was the unrivaled authority in Buddhist thought. In particular, the content of *Treatise on the Awakening of Faith in the Mahayana* was so remarkable that Buddhist monks in China employed it as a textbook for student monks and frequently referenced it in their writings.

"The Sentient Being that Ought to be Liberated is Here..." Master Dae-Ahn Rebukes Master Wonhyo

One day, returning to Boonhwangsa Temple from an outing, Master Wonhyo met Master Dae-Ahn, an older monk. Master Dae-Ahn was an unconventional Buddhist monk whose appearance was no different from that of a layman. He greeted Master Wonhyo warmly saying, "Master Wonhyo, your books have great depth." With this compliment, he asked Master Wonhyo if he had time to talk. Master Dae-Ahn was not highly regarded within the Shilla Buddhist circles, but Master Wonhyo was well aware that the old monk had attained a high level of enlightenment, so he readily agreed to talk with him and followed him. Behind Boonhwangsa Temple flowed Bookcheon River, and across the river, there was a run-down village called "Boogok" or "Soh," inhabited by some of the poorest and lowest class people in Shilla. Dae-Ahn took Master Wonhyo to the village. It was the first time that Master Wonhyo had ever visited a slum, because as a young Hwarang, he led the life of a nobleman, and after he became a monk, spent his days in Buddhist temples, so he had no reason to ever go to a slum. Master Wonhyo thought that a slum was a dirty and corrupt place, so he did not want to follow Master Dae-Ahn into the village. However, because he knew that "everything is created by the mind," he changed his mind and entered the slum. Master Dae-Ahn took him to a tavern and said to the owner, "I brought an important guest. Bring us strong drinks and something to eat." To Master Wonhyo, this was unacceptable behavior for a Buddhist monk, so he walked out of the tavern. Master Dae-Ahn hurriedly called after him, "Master Wonhyo, Master Wonhyo!" But, Master Wonhyo did not look back. As he was walking away from the tavern, he heard Master Dae-Ahn shout out, "Master Wonhyo! The sentient being that ought to be liberated is here. Why are you looking for him elsewhere?"

Master Dae-Ahn's words shook Master Wonhyo to the core. The main principle of Mahayana Buddhism is the liberation of sentient beings by bodhisattvas. Master Wonhyo had earned his reputation through his notable theories and interpretations of Mahayana Buddhist thoughts. Back at the temple, when he sat down to think about Master Dae-Ahn's words, he painfully realized that his actions contradicted his beliefs. His insight and logic were on the right path, but his actions did not follow. Even after becoming aware that nothing is actually dirty or clean and that the mind creates everything, he had been reluctant to enter a slum because he thought it was dirty and had walked out of the tavern because he thought it was corrupt.

Such actions were not consistent with the Buddha's teachings. He clearly realized, "Ah, I still have a long way to go. I may have understood the teachings, but they are not being translated into actions in my everyday life."

Soon after, Master Wonhyo abandoned his role as an instructor of Buddhist monks and stopped teaching and writing. After letting his hair grow, and with his identity hidden behind layman's clothes, he took a job as a menial worker in a Buddhist temple and served student monks. Master

Wonhyo, who had been a teacher to monks, changed his appearance and became a servant to young monks, making their meals and heating their rooms. One of the menial workers mistreated Master Wonhyo, but Master Wonhyo always treated him warmly and respectfully, in the manner of a bodhisattva.

In the temple lived an old hunchback monk whom everyone called "Bangwool Sunim." This monk did not eat his meal with the other monks at meal times. He always came to the kitchen after the meal was over while people were doing the dishes, and asked for "nuroongji." * As a result, the menial workers looked down on him and

* Hard and crunchy overcooked rice remaining at the bottom of the pot.

made fun of him. Regardless of such treatment, Bangwool Sunim continued to ask for "nuroongji" and smiled happily at everyone he met. Master Wonhyo felt sorry for him, and took good care of him.

Good-Bye, Wonhyo

One day, Master Wonhyo was listening to young student monks talking amongst themselves while he was sweeping. These young monks were studying "Inspiring Yourself to Practice" written by Master Wonhyo, and they were talking about him.

"Master Wonhyo is truly brilliant. Have you ever met him?"

"I have never met him."

"Where can you find him?"

"I heard he lives at Boonghwangsa Temple."

"Well, I heard that he is no longer there. He left suddenly without a word to anyone."

These young monks could not have guessed in their wildest dreams that Master Wonhyo, whom they admired so much, was the menial worker who ran their errands.

One day soon after, some upper class student monks were debating on the core thought of Mahayana Buddhism while studying their textbook, *The Awakening of Faith in the Mahayana*. Master Wonhyo, who was mopping the wooden floor nearby, was listening to their debate, and found what they were saying was wide of the mark. Thus, momentarily forgetting his adopted identity, he cut into the debate and

corrected them. The student monks were outraged.

"How dare a menial worker think he knows better than a monk?" cried the young monks angrily. Realizing his big blunder, he begged them for forgiveness, saying, "I don't know what came over me. I think I was momentarily insane. Please forgive me." Thus, he barely managed to stave off a crisis.

After this incident, the student monks went to their teacher and told him that *The Awakening of Faith in the Mahayana* was too difficult for them. The teacher thus handed them *Treatise on the Awakening of Faith in the Mahayana*, which was also written by Master Wonhyo, telling them to study it. When they read it, they found it both profound and easy to understand. Also, the content of the book was exactly the same as what the crazy menial worker had told them. Consequently, they became a little suspicious of the identity of the worker.

Feeling that his identity might soon be revealed, Master Wonhyo decided to leave the temple. He packed his bags after everyone in the temple had fallen asleep. He was quietly leaving through the gate when the door to Bangwool Sunim's room opened and a voice said, "Good-bye, Wonhyo!" Upon hearing these words, Master Wonhyo was struck by a clear realization.

Free from Discriminatory Thoughts, Master Wonhyo Returns to the Slum

On the one hand, the monks at the temple did not recognize Master Wonhyo while he was aware of their every move and progress in their studies. On the other hand, although Master Wonhyo did not truly know Bangwool Sunim, Bangwool Sunim had seen right through him. He had been observing Master Wonhyo serve the monks and cater to their unreasonable demands in the manner of a bodhisattva. He had also observed silently as Master Wonhyo humbly endured the mistreatment from senior menial workers. Furthermore, he had tried to provoke Master Wonhyo with nonsensical remarks, and sometimes had made unreasonable requests to have a meal prepared for him after all the dishes had been done. However, Master Wonhyo, feeling sorry for him, had always treated him courteously.

Although Master Wonhyo might have felt sorry for Bangwool Sunim, Bangwool Sunim was actually a wise monk who had attained a higher level of enlightenment than Master Wonhyo. Master Wonhyo had not been able to see Bangwool Sunim as he truly was, but Bangwool

Sunim had known exactly who Master Wonhyo was. Being oblivious to this fact, Master Wonhyo had pitied Bangwool Sunim and had worked hard to liberate "poor Bangwool Sunim."

The words, "Good-bye, Wonhyo!," helped Master Wonhyo become free of the illusion he had been under. Now, he finally understood the true meaning of Master Dae-Ahn's words. At the time, Master Wonhyo thought they meant, 'Sitting at your desk, you talk about liberating sentient beings, but how do you think you can do that if you discriminate and ignore the people living in this slum? What you say is nothing more than a desk theory.' Also, he had interpreted what Master Dae-Ahn told him as, 'If you truly are a bodhi-sattva, you should come to the slum and liberate the people by teaching them and helping them obtain enlightenment. What kind of a bodhisattva refuses to come here for the sake of his fame and prestige and even runs away from this place in fear?' Thus, Master Wonhyo had repented his actions, and had come to work at the temple as a menial worker in order to live the life of a bodhisattva. Now he realized he had misinterpreted Master Dae-Ahn's words.

Who was Master Dae-Ahn talking about when he said, "The sentient being that ought to be liberated is here..."? He was talking about Master Wonhyo who had been discriminatory about what he encountered in the slum, thinking, 'This is right; this is wrong; this is clean; this is dirty; a monk shouldn't go into a tavern...' He was rebuking Master Wonhyo by saying, "You, being so discriminatory at this very moment, are the sentient being, yet you are searching for him elsewhere." Master Wonhyo realized that Master Dae-Ahn had been telling him the sentient being was none other than him, who was creating discriminatory thoughts. That is, endless discriminatory thoughts and emotional afflictions in fact create sentient beings. Master Wonhyo had thought he already knew the meaning of "everything is created by the mind." However, only now did he finally obtain complete enlightenment of its meaning. He at last realized that the mind creates Buddhas and sentient beings. It was because he viewed the world with such discriminatory eyes that he had not recognized countless enlightened people in the world. Also, he had been under the misconception that the low class people living in the slum were the sentient beings that he, the bodhisattva, had to liberate.

Master Wonhyo realized that Master Dae-Ahn lived in the slum not because he took pity on the low class people and wanted to liberate them but because, being free from discriminatory perception, he regarded them as his friends and even teachers.

Upon this realization, Master Wonhyo went back to the slum. This time he did not go there to liberate the residents, because he no longer made the distinction between himself and others, or thought of liberating them. He went back to the slum to live among the low class people, regarding

them as his teachers and companions in his path to a higher level of enlightenment.

However, Master Wonhyo met an unexpected obstacle when he went to live in the slum. The villagers revered him as "the Great Master Wonhyo." Master Wonhyo had let go of all his discriminatory thoughts, but the low class people treated him with reverence. He went back to the slum to befriend them as their equal, but that was not possible since they regarded him as someone superior to them. In the past he could not become their friend because he had looked down on them, but this time he could not do so as they looked up to him as a great monk.

Master Wonhyo thought deeply to himself. 'Does the problem lie with me or with the village people?' If he discriminated against or looked down upon them, it would be his fault, but that was not the case. 'I have completely opened my heart to them, but their hearts remain closed to me. I can't do anything about that.' However, he soon realized that the problem lay with him because the renowned name, "Master Wonhyo," was causing them to behave that way toward him.

Master Wonhyo Becomes Sohseong Guhsa*

Master Wonhyo rid himself of his famous name by creating a public scandal with Princess Yoseok. After the scandal, the royal families, the noblemen, and Buddhist monks of Shilla all denounced him

* Buddhist layman is called "Guhsa" in Korea.

for "breaking the precepts," and they turned their backs on him. The great teacher became an outcast overnight. While the people living in the slum were marginalized because of their low social status, Master Wonhyo was ostracized from the Buddhist circles as well as the prevalent Buddhist mainstream society because he violated a Buddhist precept.

This time, when Master Wonhyo went back to the slum as an outcast, the people in the slum willingly accepted him as their friend. He was finally able to live among them as their equal. There was no apparent trace of the Great Master Wonhyo left in him. From then on, Master Wonhyo called himself Sohseong Guhsa and associated with thugs, drunks, thieves, and snake hunters. The great Buddhist monk, Master Wonhyo, no longer existed. However, the people he associated with gradually began changing: thieves no longer stole; hunters no longer killed; thugs no longer assaulted; and drunks no longer drank. He can be compared to a bodhisattva who appears in a billion different embodiments according to each situation to liberate "sentient beings." This is "Hwajak," the highest stage of practice.

There is little record in the *Memorabilia of the Three Korean Kingdoms* about Master Wonhyo after he began living as Sohseong Guhsa. One record that remains to date is a conversation between Master Wonhyo and his friend Sadong, a snake hunter. One day, Sadong's mother passed away. At the time, the low class people were prohibited from burying their dead in a coffin or making a tomb, so they either left the bodies in a forest or buried them in an unmarked place. Sadong asked Master Wonhyo to help him bury his mother. After wrapping the body with matting, the two went up the mountain, one carrying the head and the other the legs on his shoulder. While burying the body at the foot of the mountain, Sadong said to Master Wonhyo, "You were a monk once. Could you chant something to wish she be reborn in heaven?" Master Wonhyo agreed and recited a simple verse.

Do not be born;
dying causes suffering.

Do not die;

being born causes suffering.

Although Buddhist monks usually chant, shaking their hand bells for at least an hour or two during a funeral, Master Wonhyo chanted this short verse. However, Sadong thought even that was too long and said, "That' s too long. Make it short." So, Master Wonhyo chanted, "Living and dying both cause suffering." Upon hearing it, Sadong smiled with satisfaction. Then, he and Master Wonhyo walked down the mountain. Their relationship was one of equality rather than one in which one taught or bound the other.

If we view Master Wonhyo' s life in light of the four stages of practice, the period of Hwarang in his youth belongs to the first stage. The period in which he practiced fearlessly to attain enlightenment after becoming a monk corresponds to the second stage. The period following the enlightenment that "everything is created by the mind," which he attained after drinking water from a skull, is the third stage. Finally, his life after breaking the precept and returning to the slum is comparable to the fourth stage of practice. He had gone through the different levels of practice and had attained the highest level of enlightenment to become a Buddha.

AN AWAKENED LIFE

That life is like a dream does not mean that our lives are futile or that "life is but an empty dream." Just as the burglar, who was chasing you in your dream, does not actually exist once you wake up, no real joy, anger, sorrow or pleasure exists in our lives.

It is your mind that draws a picture of joy, anger, sorrow or pleasure.

Likewise, you may say, "He or she is a good or bad person," or "That is why this is happening."

But what you say is simply a discriminatory thought coming from your karma.

Just as there is nothing real in a dream, the

discriminatory thought of something being "right or wrong" is only a dream. There is no reason for you to hold onto such a thought because the notion of right or wrong is a mere dream your mind creates.

To be free from this discriminatory illusion, always be awake as if you have just woken up from a dream.

It is your mind that creates the feelings of sorrow and pain on its own. Even if you are diagnosed with cancer, it won't be a problem unless you allow yourself to be troubled by it.

The mind itself is the source of your problem

That is why I say, "Wake up from the delusion the mind creates just as you would wake up from a dream."

Absolute Freedom:
Letting Go of the Form of Self

Insisting on a Certain Condition Allows Only Partial Freedom

We demand freedom because we think that freedom is something we must obtain. Why do we demand freedom? What is freedom? The common meaning of having "freedom" is doing whatever we want to do.

At school, there are many occasions in which the entire class goes to watch a movie together with their teacher. When the teacher announces, "We are going to the movies today," most students are happy about it, but some students are not. One student may say to the teacher, "I don't want to go to the movies." However, the teacher will ignore the remark, telling the student that the entire class is required to go. If the student still doesn't want to go to the movies, he will plead, saying, "I have the right not to go to the movies."

Let's look at a different scenario. The same student is studying at home and suddenly feels like going to the movies. He asks his mother for permission, but she doesn't allow him to go, telling him to study instead. He may keep pestering his mother to let him go to the movies. If she doesn't budge, what do you think he will say? He will very likely say, "I have the right to go to the movies."

This student claims "his right to go to the movies" when he is not allowed to go because he has to study and asserts "his right not to go to the movies" when he is required to go to the movies with his class. What is freedom to this student? To him, freedom is not going to the movies when he doesn't want to and going to the movies when he does. At the root of his actions is the thought "freedom is being able to do whatever I want to do."

This common notion of liberty actually limits people's freedom. In reality, we have both the freedom to go and not go to the movies. We have the right to smoke and not to smoke. When you are listening to a dharma talk, you are not being deprived of the freedom to smoke but enjoying the freedom not to smoke. If someone threatens you at gun point and orders, "Smoke!," there is no reason for you to insist on not smoking. You should simply enjoy the freedom to smoke.

People who insist on smoking, no matter what, are deprived of their right to smoke if they run out of cigarettes. Those who insist on not smoking will be deprived of "their freedom not to smoke" when faced with a situation in which they have to smoke.

Letting Go of the Thought that Everything Must Go Your Way Leads to Unhindered Freedom

People have true freedom when they are unhindered by external conditions. They can enjoy the right to smoke when it is required of them, and

they can enjoy the right not to smoke when
smoking is not allowed. When we reach the state
of total freedom, we can be happy whether or not
we fall into the sea. That is, if we are thrust into
the sea by a big wave, we can enjoy the freedom
to collect clams; and if we do not fall into the sea
thanks to good weather, we can enjoy the freedom

to ride a boat.

It is the same with marriages. People who are already married are enjoying the freedom to be married, and those who are yet to be married are enjoying the freedom not to be married. If you realize this, you can enjoy absolute freedom, the kind of freedom no one can take away from you.

You need to let go of the thought that things must go your way. As long as you hold onto this thought, it is impossible for you to enjoy unhindered freedom. The phrase "there is nothing to be obtained" appears in *the Heart Sutra*. People need to realize that freedom is not something to be obtained. If they let go of the thought of obtaining freedom, they can stop struggling for it.

Here is an example. If someone swears at you,

you usually swear back at him or her. This is how people in the first category behave. Those in the second category avoid meeting people who swear at them. Those in the third category do not get angry even if others swear at them. Finally, those in the fourth category can swear back, if needed, at the people who swear at them. Outwardly, it might seem like the people in the first and fourth categories are the same, but they are completely different. Those in the first category cannot help getting angry if they are sworn at and cannot stop themselves from swearing back. However, those in the fourth category are enjoying their freedom to swear back, and are using the act of swearing as a way to enlighten others. If they ever instinctively swear back at others based on an emotional reaction like those in the first category, they quickly realize, "Aha, I reacted emotionally; I still have a long way to go in my practice." Then, they are right back in the fourth level.

We shouldn't feel embarrassed about not knowing something. If there is something we don't know, we can learn it; if we make a mistake, we can correct it; and if we do something wrong, we can repent. To become like the people in the third category, one needs to have great self-control and not be affected by any external conditions. This is not necessary for those in the fourth category, because they have already let go of the "self" they were holding onto.

Let's say, someone heard me swear. Then that person might ask, "How can a Buddhist monk

swear?" If I were holding onto the thought that "I am a Buddhist monk," I would be embarrassed. If I answered "Buddhist monks can swear. We are people too," I would be defending myself. However, if I responded with "Oh, I lost my temper for an instant. I am so sorry," acknowledging my mistake, and apologized, I would not be embarrassed or hurt by the incident. Rather, it would provide an opportunity to advance my practice.

Practicing to Become a Bodhisattva: Being Aware of One's State of Mind

How should school teachers practice to reach the third or the fourth stage? They shouldn't be uncomfortable about the students asking questions in class. Those in the first category are flustered when they cannot answer a difficult question a student asks. Those in the fourth category are unfazed even if they don' t know the answer to a student' s question. They explain what they know, and if they don' t know, they honestly say, "I don' t know the answer. I will look it up or ask another teacher, and I will give you the answer tomorrow." They will come back to the class the next day and tell the student what they learned about the question from another teacher or books. They are likely to tell the student, "That was a good question. If you had not asked me the question, I would not have thought to look it up. Thanks to you, I have learned something new." If teachers are always ready to learn, it' s not a problem that they don't know the answer to a question.

If teachers respond to situations in which they don't know the answer with "How can I know everything?" and move on to another subject, they are behaving in a way typical of the people in the first level of practice. These teachers are holding onto the thought that teachers should know the answers to all the questions the students might ask. As a result, they feel embarrassed when faced with a question they cannot answer. According to their way of thinking, this problem can only be solved by studying hard and acquiring enough knowledge to answer any questions that may come their way.

The teachers in the fourth level of practice are

unfazed even if they don't know the answer to a question. It's not a problem for them because they will use the opportunity to learn something new and advance their practice. This is possible because they have let go of the thought of "self" and no longer have their defenses up.

Teachers should aim for the fourth level of

practice. If you observe yourself being flustered upon receiving a difficult question, you should quickly realize, 'This behavior belongs to people in the first category.' If you see yourself ignoring the question and trying to get out of the situation by changing the subject, you should think, 'I am like those in the second category.' Then, if you feel confident about answering any questions from students, you will know 'I am aspiring to be like those in the third category.' Only if you become like those in the fourth category will you have true freedom.

Insisting on a certain thing hinders freedom. Having absolute freedom is not holding onto "self" as demonstrated by water. Water does not have a fixed form, so it changes according to the shape of the bowl it is in. We practice to arrive at the state of true freedom, and this practice is not very difficult.

Practicing to Become a Bodhisattva: Regular Repentance

Repentance is a very important part of practice. The reason we have feelings of sadness and hurt in our hearts is that we think, 'What I did is right. I am right.' Because we think we are right, we expect others to acknowledge it. However, this is not always the case. As a result, we feel anger and hatred toward them. We want to have our own way, but as this is not always possible, we become indignant. If we change our thinking to 'I am lacking. I have been unwise,' and let go of the thought that we are right, the hurt and anger in our hearts will disappear instantly.

Therefore, it is very important to take the time to repent. If we repent our wrongdoings on a regular basis, the negative emotions in our hearts will not last long. Although we may not be able to let go of the pain right away despite our repentance, it will eventually become possible. With practice, letting go of our worst hurt will not take more than a few days.

Who suffers the most when we hate others? We do. The person who gets angry and irritated is the one who suffers. We can become happy and let go of our hurt through repentance. Keep practicing this way. Thinking about who-did-what-to-whom is not repentance. Rather, repentance is realizing

once again that "nothing in the world is wrong or right." Suffering is created because we hold onto the thought that we are right. However, there is nothing wrong or right, so we need to let go of that thought. Only then can we begin the journey to serenity, happiness, and freedom. With continuous repentance, our sense of injury disappears. If we realize that we are no more significant in this world than a bunch of grass by the street, nothing can hurt our feelings. It is because we think we are special beings that conflicts are created and feelings are hurt.

Practicing to Become a Bodhisattva: Letting Go of "Self"

People who are not self-defensive will respond readily when someone asks them to sing, even though they might be such poor singers that they only know how to sing a children's song. However, self-defensive people refuse when asked to sing, even going as far as to say, "It's true. I have never sung a song in my life." If others still insist that they sing, self-defensive people will reluctantly begin to sing. They usually sing a classic song or some other type of refined tune, and they usually turn out to be pretty good singers.

Why do they behave that way? When self-defensive people are asked to sing, they don't readily agree because they are obsessed with the thought of "doing things well." Sometimes, their voices begin to tremble for fear that someone might think, 'He or she is such a bad singer.' They become obsessed with such thoughts because they think of themselves as special beings.

You need to know that a special social position is a barrier for your practice. When people seek you out, pamper you, and revere you, you are likely to let these things go to your head. Thus, you may be deluded into thinking that you are an extraordinary person. If that happens, who loses out and becomes miserable? You do, of course.

People who do not know how to love themselves commit such folly. You should always be aware you are not special in any way. Your life will be completely ruined the moment you are deluded into thinking you are an exceptional person just because people seek you out and think highly of you. Here lies the reason we need to pray every day.

Praying every day helps us be awake at each and every moment, so that even if we are influenced by external conditions, we can quickly stop ourselves from being affected any further. All of us are constantly reacting to circumstances as evidenced by how we get angry when someone criticizes us or get elated when someone praises us.

Practice is a way to make oneself complete. It is also not having a fixed form of oneself. Figuratively speaking, if you think of yourself as insignificant as a wild flower growing on the side of the road, rather than feeling hopeless and empty, you are likely to feel content wherever you are, whomever you meet, and whatever you do.

You must let go of the thought that you must become someone. How other people think of you and treat you are based on their own perspective, so you must not let them affect you. If you lead your life your own way, practicing diligently, others will eventually admire and respect you. If you still think of yourself as an insignificant person, others will praise you for your humility, even though you are not especially trying to be humble.

We practice to become such a person. If you have true freedom, your ability will be employed where it' s needed the most, even if you don' t particularly try to help others. So, please, keep on practicing diligently.

One afternoon in the early winter of 1969, with a feeling of haste during the final exam period, he bowed to the Buddha statue in the Main Dharma Hall and was about to leave the temple.

Then, the Abbot called him.

"Dear Abbot, I am busy today."

"Oh, you are busy today?"

"Yes. I have exams tomorrow."

"Where did you come from?"

"I came from school."

"Where were you before school?"

"I was at home."

"Where were you before you were at home?"

"........."

"WHERE WERE YOU BEFFORE YOU WERE AT HOME?

"I was in my mother's womb."

"Where were you before you were in your mom's womb?"

"I don' t know."

"Where are you going?"

"I am going home."

"Okay. Where will you go after you get home?"

"I have to go to school."

"Where will you go after school?"

".........."

"WHERE WILL YOU GO AFTER SCHOOL?"

"I will die."

"After you die, where will you go?"

"I don't know. How should I know where I will be going after I die?"

"YOU STUPID BOY! How come an IDIOT who doesn't know even where he came from and where he is going is so BUSY?"

"How come I am so busy when I don't even know where I came from and where I will go?" This koan (or Kongan in Korean) led Ven. Pomnyun Sunim to a monastic life and eventually to becoming a monk. Since then, Ven. Pomnyun Sunim has completely enlightened his life with the Buddha's teachings. Based on these teachings, he offers guidance whereby many illuminate their lives.

Ven. Pomnyun Sunim is the founder and guiding Zen master of Jungto Society in South Korea. He is not only a Buddhist monk and Zen master but also a social activist who leads various movements such as ecological awareness campaigns; promotion of human rights and world peace; and eradication of famine, disease, and illiteracy.

As the motto of Jungto Society, "Pure Mind, Good Friends, and Clean Land," demonstrates, Ven. Pomnyun Sunim has been advocating a new paradigm of civilization in which everyone is happy through practice, creates a congenial society through active participation in social movements, and protects the environment and the Earth through a simple lifestyle.

Jungto Society has been working to create a community that enables its members to view the difficulties people face today from a global perspective and to play a leading role in solving these problems. As of 2011, Jungto Society consists of 18 regional chapters in Korea and 19 overseas chapters

* Buddhist monk is called "Sunim" in Korean.

including 7 in the United States.

As part of the new paradigm movement, Ven. Pomnyun Sunim founded Join Together Society in 1994 to eradicate famine in developing countries; EcoBuddha in 1994 to protect the environment; and Good Friends in 1999 to push for human rights, help refugees, and bolster world peace. He also established The Peace Foundation, a private research institute, in 2004, to bring permanent peace, stability, and unification to the Korean peninsula. Through these organizations, he has devoted himself to advocating human rights, fighting famine, disease, and illiteracy in many countries (Afghanistan, India, Mongolia, Myanmar, Philippines, Sri Lanka, and North Korea), in addition to promoting peace on the Korean peninsula.

In recognition of his efforts to champion peace and human rights, Ven. Pomnyun Sunim was presented the Ramon Magsaysay Award for Peace and International Understanding in September 2002.

Books and Commentaries

English

True Happiness

Japanese

My Happy Way to Work

French

Familly

Korean

The Way to the Unification of the Korean Peninsula
The Harmony of Work and Buddhist Practice
Looking for Happiness in the World
  - In Search of a Hopeful Paradigm for Society
New Leadership for Future Generations
Buddhism and Peace
Buddhism and Environment
Commentaries I and II on the Diamond Sutra
Commentary on the Heart Sutra
The Frog Jumped Out of a Well
A Treatise for Young Buddhist Practitioners
Buddha - The Life and Philosophy
Engaged Buddhism
Eastern Philosophy and Environmental Issues
Prayer

Awards

1998 Kyobo Environmental Education Award, Korea
2000 Manhae Propagation Award,Korea
2002 Ramon Magsaysay Peaceand International Understanding Award, Philippines
2006 DMZ(DemilitarizedZone) Peace Prize, Gangwon Province, Korea.
2007 National Reconciliationand Cooperation Award, Korean Council for
      Reconciliation and Cooperation, Korea